Dear Parents:

Congratulations! Your child is taking the first steps on an exciting journey. The destination? Independent reading!

STEP INTO READING® will help your child get there. The program offers five steps to reading success. Each step includes fun stories and colorful art or photographs. In addition to original fiction and books with favorite characters, there are Step into Reading Non-Fiction Readers, Phonics Readers and Boxed Sets, Sticker Readers, and Comic Readers—a complete literacy program with something to interest every child.

Learning to Read, Step by Step!

Ready to Read **Preschool–Kindergarten**
• big type and easy words • rhyme and rhythm • picture clues
For children who know the alphabet and are eager to begin reading.

Reading with Help **Preschool–Grade 1**
• basic vocabulary • short sentences • simple stories
For children who recognize familiar words and sound out new words with help.

Reading on Your Own **Grades 1–3**
• engaging characters • easy-to-follow plots • popular topics
For children who are ready to read on their own.

Reading Paragraphs **Grades 2–3**
• challenging vocabulary • short paragraphs • exciting stories
For newly independent readers who read simple sentences with confidence.

Ready for Chapters **Grades 2–4**
• chapters • longer paragraphs • full-color art
For children who want to take the plunge into chapter books but still like colorful pictures.

STEP INTO READING® is designed to give every child a successful reading experience. The grade levels are only guides; children will progress through the steps at their own speed, developing confidence in their reading. The F&P Text Level on the back cover serves as another tool to help you choose the right book for your child.

Remember, a lifetime love of reading starts with a single step!

For the Violet Femmes
—A.M.

For Karlos
—T.B.

Visit us on the Web!
StepIntoReading.com
rhcbooks.com

Educators and librarians, for a variety of teaching tools, visit us at RHTeachersLibrarians.com

Library of Congress Cataloging-in-Publication Data
Names: Membrino, Anna, author. | Budgen, Tim, illustrator.
Title: Big Shark, Little Shark, Baby Shark / written by Anna Membrino ;
illustrated by Tim Budgen.
Description: First edition. | New York : Random House Children's Books, [2020] |
Series: Step into reading. Step 1 |
Audience: Ages 4–6 | Audience: Grades K–1 | Summary: "What happens when Mommy Shark, Daddy Shark, Grandpa Shark and Grandma Shark find out that Big Shark and Little Shark are avoiding Baby Shark?" —Provided by publisher.
Identifiers: LCCN 2019026493 (print) | LCCN 2019026494 (ebook) |
ISBN 978-0-593-12809-1 (trade pbk.) | ISBN 978-0-593-12810-7 (lib. bdg.) |
ISBN 978-0-593-12811-4 (ebook)
Subjects: CYAC: Sharks—Fiction. | Brothers and sisters—Fiction. | Play—Fiction.
Classification: LCC PZ7.M5176 Bk 2020 (print) | LCC PZ7.M5176 (ebook) | DDC [E]—dc23

Printed in the United States of America
10 9 8 7 6 5 4 3 2 1
First Edition

This book has been officially leveled by using the F&P Text Level Gradient™ Leveling System.

STEP INTO READING®

Big Shark, Little Shark, Baby Shark

by Anna Membrino

illustrated by Tim Budgen

Random House New York

Big shark.
Little shark.

Big Shark and
Little Shark are friends.

They are at the
Shark Park.

They play games.
They have fun!

Oh no.

Here comes
Baby Shark.

Big Shark and
Little Shark
do NOT want to play
with Baby Shark.

Baby Shark
is too little.
Baby Shark
is too slow.

It is NOT fun
to play with
Baby Shark!

Big Shark and
Little Shark
swim away.

Baby Shark is sad.

Baby Shark swims
to Mommy Shark
and Daddy Shark.

They are mad
at Big Shark and
Little Shark.

Mommy Shark tells
Grandpa Shark
what Big Shark
and Little Shark did.

Grandpa Shark tells
Grandma Shark
what Big Shark
and Little Shark did.

The family of sharks is mad!

What will they do?

All five sharks
take a deep breath.

They will play
their own game!

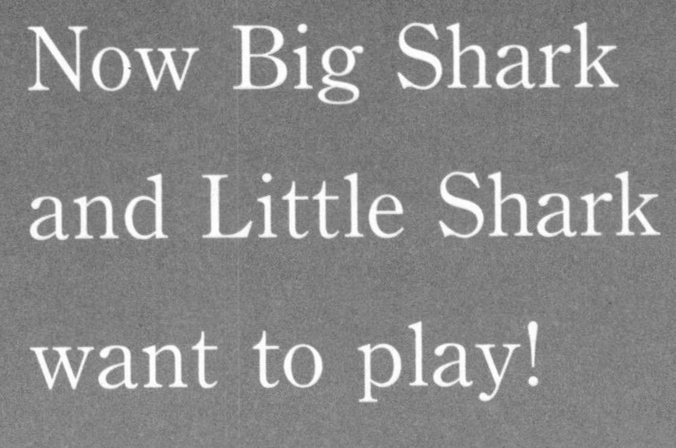
Now Big Shark
and Little Shark
want to play!

They say
they are sorry
for not being kind.

Baby Shark
asks them to play, too.

They all play
shark baseball
together!